Night Fishing

Marian Iseard

Published in association with
The Basic Skills Agency

Hodder & Stoughton

A MEMBER OF THE HODDER HEADLINE GROUP

Acknowledgements
Cover: Barry Downard
Illustrations: Doug Gray

Orders: please contact Bookpoint Ltd, 130 Milton Park, Abingdon, Oxon OX14 4SB. Telephone: (44) 01235 827720, Fax: (44) 01235 400454. Lines are open from 9.00 - 6.00, Monday to Saturday, with a 24 hour message answering service. You cna also order through our website www.hodderheadline.co.uk

British Library Cataloguing in Publication Data
A catalogue record for this book is available from The British Library

ISBN 0 340 81687 2

First published 2001
This edition 2003
Impression number 10 9 8 7 6 5 4 3 2 1
Year 2007 2006 2005 2004 2003

Typeset by SX Composing DTP, Rayleigh, Essex.
Printed in Great Britain for Hodder & Stoughton Educational, a division of Hodder Headline, 338 Euston Road, London NW1 3BH by Athenaeum Press, Gateshead, Tyne & Wear.

About the Play

The People

- Woody
- Ben
- Carl
- Ben's Mum
- A Tramp

What's Happening

Woody, **Ben** *and* **Carl** *have decided to spend the evening night fishing by the canal.*

Act 1

On a park bench

Woody Are you up for it then?
Ben I don't know.
Woody It'll be a good crack.
Sleeping in my dad's little hut.
Have I ever taken you there?
Ben No.
Carl I've been there. It's cool. Down by the canal.
Ben What's he want a hut there for?
Woody It's on his allotment.
There's a kettle and a little heater and everything.
And he keeps his fishing gear there.
Ben Is it big enough? For three?
Woody Just. Come on, don't be chicken.
Ben I'm not! It's just . . .
Carl What? Scared of being found out?
Ben Mum'll kill me if she gets to know.

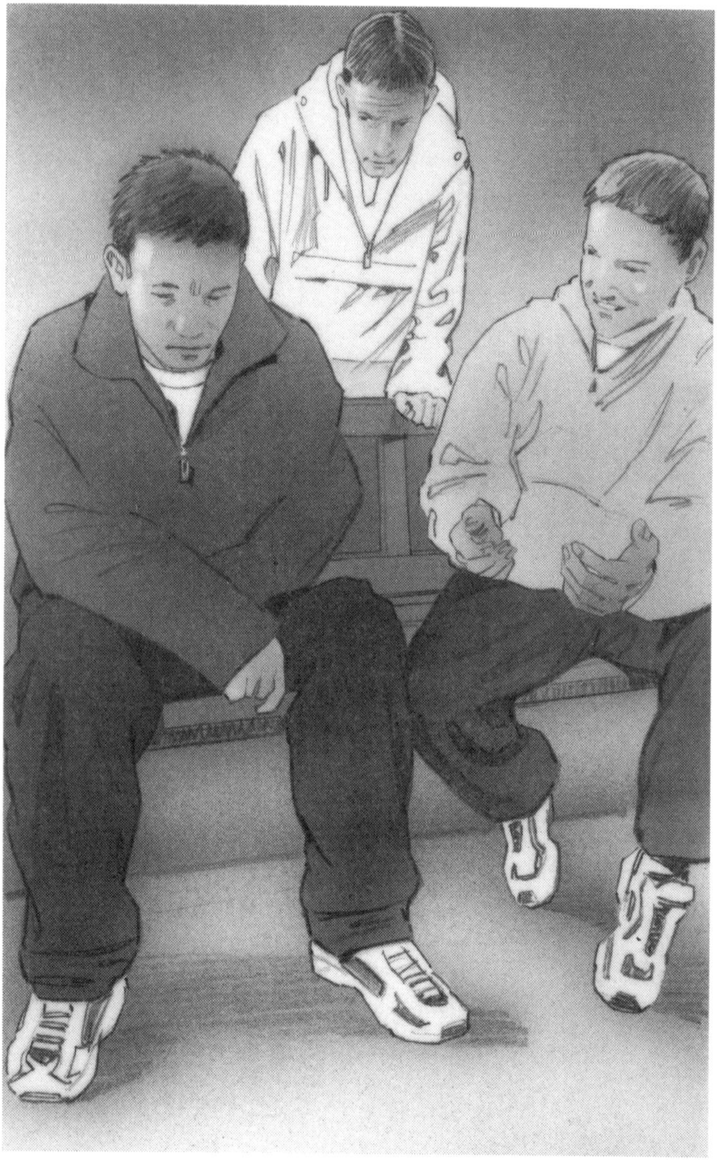

Woody Why should she?

Ben It's all right for you two.
Your parents never ring you when
you're sleeping at someone
else's house.

Carl Listen. It's easy.
You ring them on your mobile at
ten o'clock.
All you have to do is pretend
you're at Woody's house.

Woody It'll be great.
Our little hut's really cosy at night.
I stayed there with my dad once.
We did some night fishing.

Ben *(looking more interested)*
Hey, can we do that?

Woody Sure. There are two rods.
We can take it in turns.
Are you in then?

Ben OK.

Carl Great! So – I'm staying with you,
you're staying at Woody's,
and Woody's staying at mine. Right?

Woody & Ben Right!

Act 2

In **Ben***'s kitchen*
There is a sleeping-bag and rucksack on the floor.
Ben *is getting food out of the cupboard.*

Mum Why are you taking all this Ben?
Ben In case we get hungry.
Mum Doesn't Woody have food in his house?
Go easy on those biscuits.
I'm not buying any more when they've all gone.
Ben We said we'd all chip in.
Mum It looks like you're going for a month, not one night!
Ben You should see how much Woody and Carl eat!
Mum His mum must be mad.
Fancy having you three all under one roof!

Ben It's only to sleep.
We'll be down the park first.
Playing footie.

Mum Well it keeps you out of trouble
I suppose.
Do you need that sleeping-bag?

Ben Yes. Saves using theirs.

Mum Your bike will be well loaded.
You've got far too much stuff.

Ben Don't worry, Mum, I know
what I'm doing.

Mum Now then, what time are you coming
home tomorrow?

Ben I don't know, Mum.

Mum You know we're going to Auntie
Lynn's for the day.
We could pick you up on the way.
From Woody's house.

Ben *(looks very worried)*
Oh no! Don't do that! I mean – what
about my bike?

Mum We could put it in the back, if we use
Dad's van.

COKE

Ben But . . . I need to come back.
I've got lots of homework to do.
I could do some before we go out.

Mum *(looking at* **Ben** *closely)*
Homework?

Ben Yes, Mum. You know – they give it to us at school.

Mum Very funny. I was just thinking you must be ill.
Last week we had to chain you to your desk.

Ben Ha-ha.
Look, Mum, I'll come home dead early.
Before the rest of you are up.
I've got my key.

Mum All right then.
Now, don't forget to ring tonight.
Let me know when you get to Woody's house.

Ben *(escaping out the back door)*
OK. About ten o'clock. Bye, Mum.

Mum *(calls after him)*
Have you got your toothbrush?

Ben *(offstage)* Mu-um!

Act 3

The same evening, in the park, all on bikes.

Carl What have you two got to eat?

Ben Not much. My mum was in the kitchen when I left.
Watching my every move.

Woody My lot were out. I've got a pizza.
And some crisps and chocolate.

Carl I made cheese and pickle sarnies.
And I nicked some doughnuts.
I've brought some of my dad's beer too. A can each.

Ben Oh great! That was clever.

Carl What?

Ben Nicking your dad's beer.
He might ring up to find out where it's gone.

Woody Oh give it a rest, Ben!

Carl Yeah. If you're that worried don't come.
We don't want you moaning all night.

Ben OK, OK. What shall we do now?

Woody Well we can't go down to the hut yet.
There might be people still down there.
Some of them know me.
We'll have to wait until it gets dark.

Carl Let's play footie. Practise for next week's match.
Then we'll go and get some chips.

Act 4

Down by the canal, the boys are creeping along the towpath to **Woody** *'s dad's hut. It is dark and they use their bike lamps to see their way.*

Carl Ouch! Stupid nettles!

Woody Sssh! Don't make so much noise. I don't want one of my dad's mates to pop up behind the hedge.

Ben I thought you said there'd be no one here now.

Woody Well I can't say for sure, can I? I haven't got X-ray eyes.

Carl I hope your hut's in good nick. I don't fancy sleeping on a load of manure or anything.

Woody It wouldn't make much difference to the way you smell.

Carl Ha – you can talk, you've been wearing those jeans for two weeks.

Woody They're just nice and worn in now.

Carl Disgusting!

Ben How much further?

Woody Just down here. We go through this little gate.

(They go through a gate on to the allotments. They are standing next to the hut.)

Ben Brilliant!

Woody What did I tell you?
Wait till you see inside.

Carl Have you got the key?

Woody Oh no! I knew I'd forgotten something!
(he grins at their faces)
Don't be stupid, of course I've got the key.
(**Woody** *unlocks the door)*

Woody Come on. Unload your bikes and bring the stuff in.
I'll find the lamp.

(They get busy sorting things out.
Woody *gets his dad's lamp and hangs it up.)*

Carl I'm starving. Let's get the food out.

Woody You've only just had some chips.

Carl It's all this creeping about. It makes me hungry.

Ben Oh hell! What's the time?

Woody Ten past ten.

Ben I should have phoned at ten.
Mum might ring your house, Woody.

Woody Well do it now – quick.

Ben *(on phone)* Hi, Mum. It's me. Yes, I'm at Woody's.
Yes, we're having a good time.
Right, I'll see you tomorrow.
What's that?
No, I won't forget to say thank you.
Bye. *(looks at others)* Phew!

Woody OK. Now that's out of the way – let's get fishing!

Act 5

Sitting at the side of the canal,
Carl *and* **Ben** *are fishing.* **Woody** *is holding the lamp.*

Carl Does your dad ever catch anything, Woody?

Woody Sometimes. Not much.

Ben Are there any fish in here?
I bet it's too polluted.

Woody There are some. Perch mostly.

Carl I can't see the point of fishing.
You can't eat them,
when they're so small.
So what's the point?

Ben It's just a good feeling when you catch one.

Woody Talking of catching one –
you've got a bite!
Reel it in, quick.
(**Ben** *reels in a tiny fish,* **Carl** *and* **Woody** *laugh at him.)*

Carl Quick, Woody, light a fire! Ben's caught our supper!

Ben Hey, why not. Let's have a bonfire.

Woody Oh yeah, good one, Ben.
Let's tell everyone where we are.

Ben OK, it was just an idea.

Carl Woody, I think my line's got caught on something.

Woody Let's have a look.
Give me your rod.
(He tugs at the line. It's stuck fast.)
Damn! I might have to cut it.

Ben Let me have a go.

*(**Woody** gives **Ben** the rod)*

No. It's well stuck.

Woody I'll go and get my dad's knife.
He keeps it in the hut.
Trust you Carl.

Carl It wasn't my idea to go fishing.

*(**Woody** goes into the hut with the lamp.*
He comes back out with a knife.
Suddenly everything goes black.)

Carl Stop messing about, Woody.

Woody I'm not. It must be the battery that's dead.

Ben I'll get my bike lamp.

Woody I can see where you are. I'll just – aaaaagh!

Carl & Ben Woody!

Woody Aaah . . . my leg!

Carl Ben, get your bike lamp.
Quick! Shine it over here.

Ben Where? Oh God – look at his leg.

Carl He fell on the knife.
Look at all the blood!

Ben Let's get him into the hut.
We need to put something on his leg.

Carl Can you stand up, Woody?

Woody Just. But it kills.
Get me to the hut, quick.

Act 6

In the hut, the bike lamps are getting dimmer.
Woody *is lying on his sleeping-bag.*

Carl How are you feeling, Woody?
Woody Sick.
Carl Does your leg still hurt?
Woody I don't know. I can't feel it.
Ben I'm going to tie this bit of cloth round it.
It looks clean.
Carl We ought to get help.
Woody No. We'll all be in trouble then.
Carl It's better than you bleeding to death.
Woody Don't be crazy. It'll stop soon.
I'll be fine.
Ben Even if you are – what will you say to your parents tomorrow?
Woody I'll say I came off my bike.

Ben They'd never fall for that.

Woody I feel dizzy now. I feel so . . . dizzy . . .

Carl He's passed out.
We've got to do something, Ben.
I'm scared.

Ben We need to get help.

Carl One of us will have to run home.

Ben No. I can ring 999.
Where's my mobile? *(dials 999)*
Hello – we need an ambulance.
My mate's had an accident. He's cut his leg open . . .

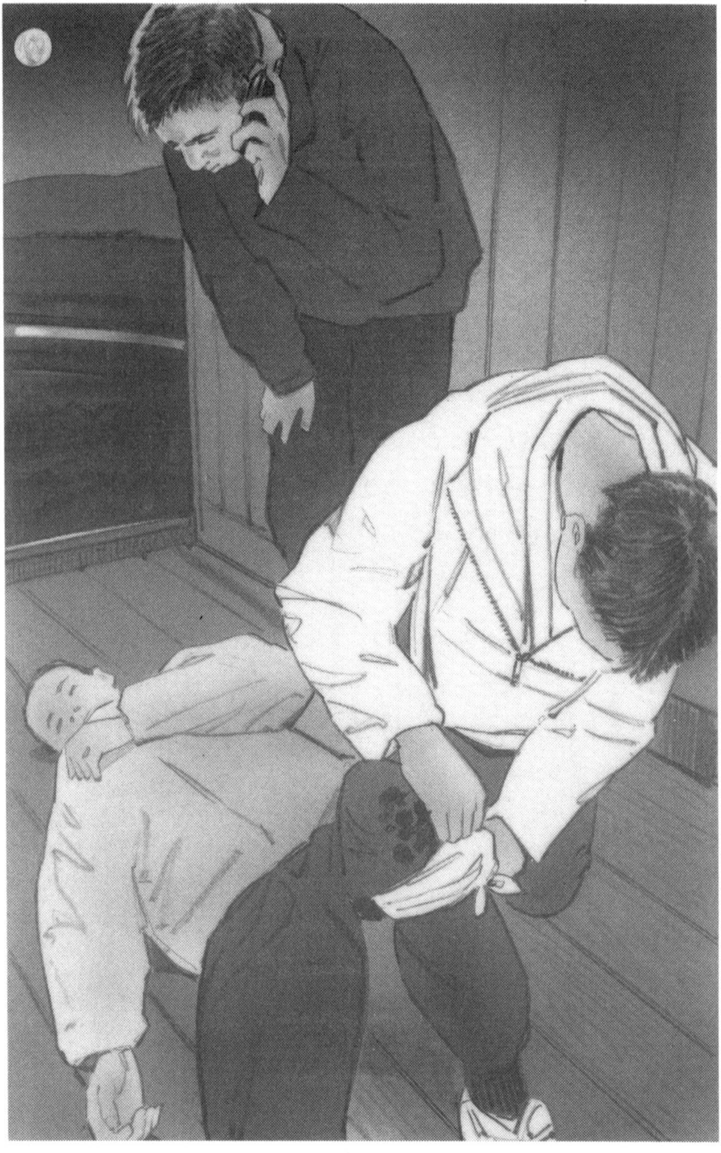

Act 7

Five minutes later, in the hut.
There is no light at all.

Carl Well, we're done for now.
Your mum and dad, and mine and Woody's.

Ben Yeah. They'll kill us.
But the ambulance people were right – we had to tell them.

Carl I wish someone would come.
Get it over with.

Ben Give them time.
It's ten minutes at least from town.

Carl What's that?

Ben What?

Carl That tapping – and rustling.
There's something out there.

Ben It's just a dog or a cat.

Carl I can hear a strange voice – muttering.
(grabs **Ben***'s arm)*
It might be a mad axeman!

Ben Don't be stupid, Carl.

Carl I'm not. It could be.
It might be an escaped prisoner.

Ben There's no prison around here.

Carl So? Madmen can walk can't they?

Ben Oh shut up! You're giving me the creeps!

(Suddenly they see a strange man's face at the window, lit up by a torch.)

Ben & Carl Aaagh!

Carl Who's that?

Ben How do I know?

Carl I don't like this.
I wish we'd never come.

Ben Well you were all for it before.
It's too late now.

Carl Listen! He's going round to the door.

Ben Quick! Lock the door!
Where's the key?

Carl Too late . . . *(the door opens)*

Tramp What's going on?
You kids shouldn't be down here.

Ben Wh . . . who are you?

Tramp Never mind that – who are you? You kids – you keep breaking into these huts.

Ben We didn't break in – this is his dad's hut. *(points to* **Woody***)*

Tramp Who? *(shines torch on* **Woody***)* Is he asleep?

Ben No, he's . . .

Carl He's not very well.

Tramp What's wrong with him?

Carl He cut his leg. Then he passed out.

Tramp Come here. Let me have a look. Blimey – there's a lot of blood here.

Ben It won't stop bleeding.

Tramp Well it won't – not with how you've tied this.

Carl What do you mean?

Tramp This bandage.
If you want to stop the bleeding you need to tie it above the cut.
(he re-ties the bandage)

Ben How do you know that?

Tramp Used to be in the army, didn't I?
A long time ago that was.
But you don't forget things like that.

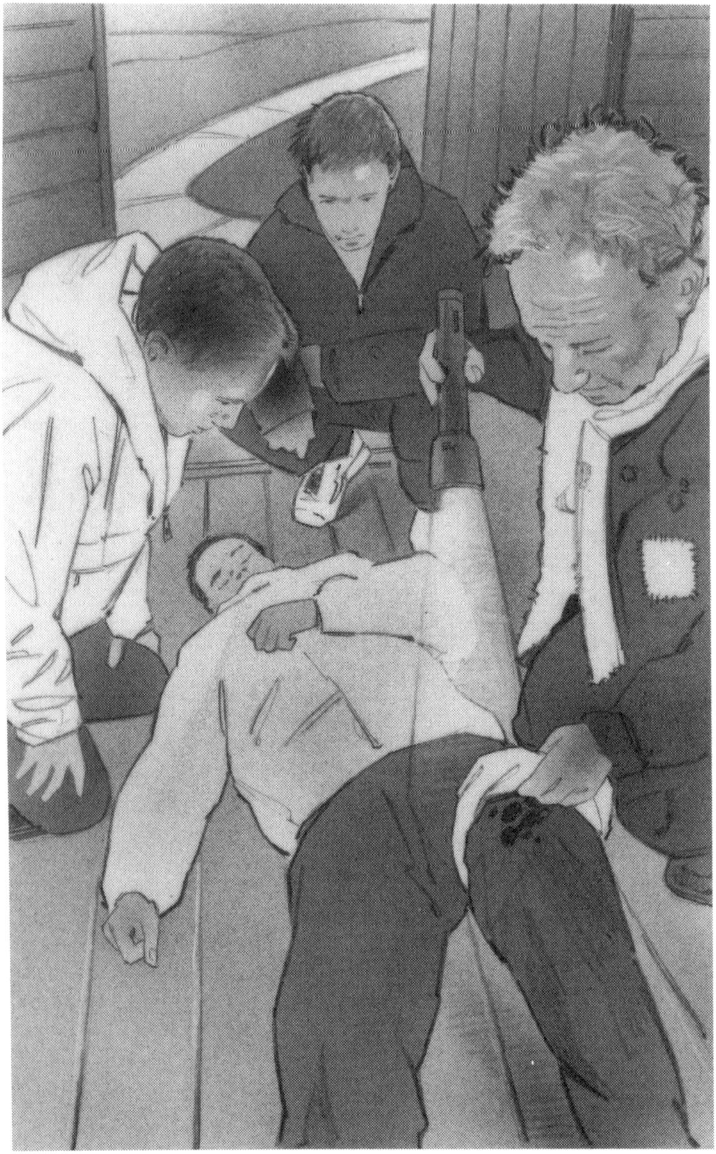

Ben Do you think he'll be all right?

Tramp He should have this seen to
by a doctor.
It needs stitches.

Carl We've rung for an ambulance.

Tramp Are you on your own?

Ben Yes.

Tramp Do your parents know where you are?

Ben They do now. And we're going to get done.

Tramp I bet you are. I dunno – kids.

Carl Listen! I can hear the ambulance.

Tramp I'll go and fetch them.
You stay here.
(he goes out)

Ben See? Mad axeman! You chicken!

Carl You were scared too, don't say you weren't.

Ben Huh – no way.

Carl Liar. Anyway, I hope he knew what he was doing.

Ben Yeah. I hope Woody's all right.
I don't care what happens now –
as long as Woody's all right.

Act 8

The next day, **Ben** *and* **Carl** *are visiting* **Woody** *at his house.*

Woody So, who was this tramp?

Ben How do we know? He just went. He didn't hang around, once the ambulance came.

Carl They said he might have saved your life.
He stopped your leg bleeding.

Woody Dad said he thinks he's seen him there before.
He used to be a major in the army.
Now he just sleeps rough.

Ben Was your dad mad?

Woody Are you joking? Mad?
I've never seen him go purple before.

Carl My mum's grounded me for a whole week.

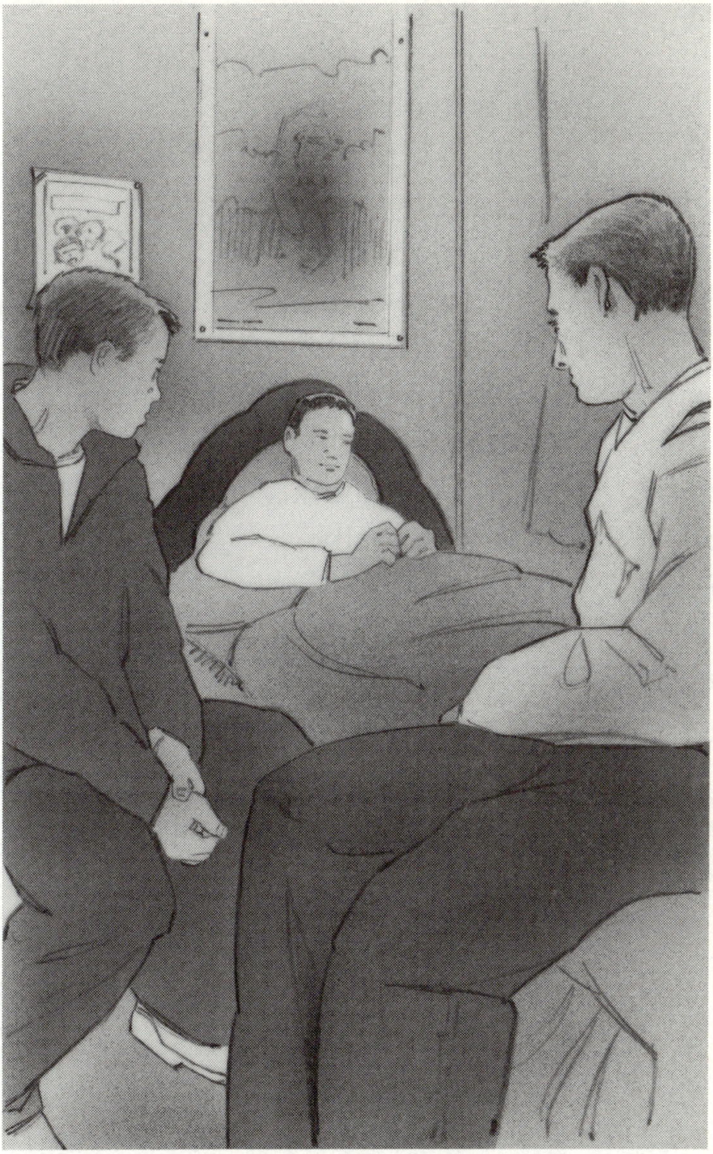

Ben You're lucky.
My mum said that, then Dad said make it two weeks.
One from him, one from her.

Carl How long before your leg gets better, Woody?

Woody About a week before I can walk on it.
There are ten stitches in it.

Ben So you won't be in the match on Saturday then?

Woody What do you think?

Carl Just as well really.

Woody Why?

Carl The match is off.

Woody Off?

Carl Yes – they've all gone down with chicken-pox.

Ben So we can't knock the spots off 'em!

Woody Ha-ha. Your jokes don't get any better do they?